SOUL SONG

SOUL SONG

L. A. WEATHERLY

Barrington Stoke

First published in 2014 in Great Britain by
Barrington Stoke Ltd
18 Walker Street, Edinburgh, EH3 7LP

www.barringtonstoke.co.uk

Copyright © 2014 L. A. Weatherly

A CIP catalogue record for this book is available
from the British Library upon request

ISBN: 978-1-78112-362-1

Printed in China by Leo

To Isabel, who knew Iris's name

How can you miss someone you've never met?

❦ 1 ❦

'Nate,' I think. 'His name is Nate, short for Nathaniel.'

I keep thinking it, over and over. I will hold on to Nate's name – the fact of him – any way I can.

Right now, it's all I have.

Dr Price sits behind a desk and watches me with keen blue eyes. "Iris, do you know why you're here?" he asks.

"Because there's been a mistake, that's why," I say. I try to sound bored – pissed off. I try not to show how scared I am.

Dr Price lifts a grey eyebrow. "But when the police officer brought you here last night, you got very upset, remember?" he asks. "You shouted, 'I trusted you!' at her. What did you mean by that?"

I shrug. Oh God, I can't believe I told that woman everything. I hate myself for being so stupid. I should have known how it would end up.

A silence falls.

Dr Price looks down at some papers. "Officer Yang says that you told her you believe some rather ... unusual things."

"I was just kidding," I say. "I didn't mean any of it!" I have a green and silver stone in my hand. I grip it hard.

Dr Price keeps on as if I hadn't spoken. "She says you told her that you've been to the past," he says. "1922, it says here. And you met a boy there who you think is your soul mate. Now the two of you are in this time – our time – together, but things aren't easy for you. Is that correct?"

Every word is correct.

"Of course it's not," I snap. "I'd have to be crazy to believe something like that."

But given where I am, I guess that is kind of the point.

Dr Price leans back and gazes at me. He clicks a pen a few times. "Officer Yang said you were very upset," he says. "Almost in tears."

I think fast. "I – I want to be an actress," I say. "I was just practising a scene."

I can tell he doesn't believe me. The chair squeaks as he sits up. "Where are your parents?" he asks.

"I don't have any."

He makes a note. "Your carers, then?"

I don't answer. If I say Texas, they'll find out I'm a runaway, for all I'm two thousand miles away in Los Angeles. There can't be *that* many runaways named Iris from Texas. And then Gary, the creep from the group home, will know where I am.

Why, why did I give that police officer my real first name?

'Nate, short for Nathaniel,' I repeat to myself. Where *is* Nate? Is he OK? I stroke my fingers over the smooth surface of the stone. It doesn't make me feel any better.

Dr Price's gaze drops down. "That's a pretty stone," he says.

I stiffen as he looks back at his notes. "You told Officer Yang that you believe it has magical powers," he says. "As long as its two halves are joined, you and this boy from the past can be in the same time together. Is that true?"

I try to look as if it doesn't matter. "It's true that I told her that," I say. "I can't believe she fell for it. Of course the stone doesn't have magical powers. There's no such thing."

Dr Price holds out his hand. "May I?"

I want to say no, but that would seem too strange. So, after a second, I give him the stone.

"Unusual," he says, as he studies it. "I've never seen anything quite like it." He watches me as he tosses it once on his palm. Its green and silver surface shimmers. "You don't believe there's anything special about it?" he asks.

I can't take my eyes off the stone. I feel cold, and I wipe my hands on my jeans. If anything happens to it …

"It's just a pretty stone, that's all," I say. My voice is faint.

Dr Price draws his hand back. "So if I were to throw it out the window ..."

"No!" I leap forward, but his fingers have closed over the stone. "Please, don't break it!" I cry. "You could ruin everything!"

A clock ticks. I shake as I sit and stare at the stone. Dr Price hands it back to me. He looks like he feels sorry for me.

"I wasn't going to harm it, Iris," he says. "But I think it's a good idea for you to stay here with us for a while. We have drugs that can help with these fantasies of yours."

Terror fills me. "I don't need help!"

He ignores me. "These fantasies have been taking over your life, haven't they?" he says. "We can help with that. But *you* have to help, too." He leans forward. "You have to work with us, Iris. We can't get you better on our own. Will you do that?"

My head pounds. 'No!' I want to shout. 'You have to let me out of here!'

Then I see the bars on the window. They're painted white to blend in with the walls, but they're still bars. I'm trapped. No one is going to believe me – no one. For now, I have to play along, until I can figure out a way to escape this place and get back to Nate.

If he still wants to have anything to do with me.

Pain stabs my heart as I think about how he must be feeling. It's all my fault.

I realise that Dr Price is waiting for an answer. I clear my throat and try to sound sincere.

"I'll help," I say.

They leave me alone for the next few hours.

The ward is depressing. Ugly. The walls are painted apple green and the sofas and chairs are brown. It's full of kids around my age. They have empty stares, or they sit and talk to themselves. They scare me, but I manage not to show it. Maybe mental illness is catching. Maybe I *will* go crazy if I don't get out of here soon.

The bedroom they give me has two single beds. The girl in the other bed is called Mel and she makes me nervous – the way she gazes into space. Sometimes she laughs out loud, as if she's watching a funny film inside her head.

I don't spend much time in the bedroom. Instead, I wander around the ward as the TV drones on in the background. I try to look as if I'm just bored and restless.

What I'm really doing is watching the front desk. There's always a nurse sitting there. The door to the ward is right beside her. A guard stands next to it. I remember from last night that there's another door beyond that one. Both doors are kept locked.

As I stare at the guard, I wonder if he keeps the keys in his pocket. Any time he looks over at me, I glance away. In the end, I give up and go back into the common area.

There is a game show on TV. There is lots of screaming and laughing coming from the screen. Here in the ward, there are just blank faces.

No one pays attention to me. I sit in the corner of a sofa and stare at the TV. The windows in here have bars on them, too.

I clench my fists. 'Nate, I'm sorry,' I think. He must be so worried about me by now, for all he was so angry before. Angrier than I've ever seen him. The thought makes me feel sick.

'Everything will be all right,' I tell him in my mind. 'I'll be back with you soon. We'll work it out.' I hope that's true. Oh God, why didn't I keep my promise to him? Why did I keep trying to find out about his family?

I lick my lips as I think about what else I found out. There's something I didn't tell Officer Yang. I'm not sure I've admitted it even to myself.

No one is watching me, so I take a postcard out of the back pocket of my jeans. I stare down at it. No, it wasn't just my imagination. My grandmother's handwriting looks fainter than it did before.

Soon it will be as if she never even existed. And when that happens ... what will it mean for me? My mother was her daughter. I can't have been born if she wasn't.

'This can't be happening,' I think as I grip the postcard. I have *got* to get back to Nate. But even if I manage to escape ... how can we fix this?

"I know why you're here," a voice hisses. I start in surprise. My room-mate Mel is sitting beside me. She's small and dark-haired, with a sharp chin like a cat.

I try not to show how nervous I am. I shove the postcard back in my pocket. "You do?" I say.

She nods. "The voices in my head tell me things," she says. "You're going to die soon, aren't you?"

❦ 2 ❧

A few days back, everything had been different.

I'd been on my feet for over ten hours at the diner where I worked. As I walked towards the bus stop, my feet hurt, and I could still smell the grease of burgers and fries. That smell was everywhere. On my hair. My skin. My clothes.

It wasn't a great job. I think the owner guessed I was a runaway, since I didn't have any I.D. He paid me in cash, and he often made me work extra hours. I couldn't say no. He might fire me, and then what would Nate and I do? We needed the money.

The air felt heavy, like it was going to rain. As I passed the library, I slowed and touched the green and silver stone in my jeans pocket. I wanted so badly to go inside and do more research. I spent time at the library whenever I could. I had to find out what had happened to Nate's family – not just for him, but for myself.

So far I hadn't had much luck. And right now, I was so tired that I felt like a zombie. I sighed and kept walking.

When I was on the bus at last, I started to feel nervous. This happened a lot now. It had been over two months since Nate and I had defeated Sybil, the evil spirit who had tried to keep us apart. But it was like part of me couldn't believe she was gone. I sat on the edge of my seat and glanced behind me, wondering if any of the other passengers were really Sybil in disguise.

No. She was dead.

But what about Gary?

Gary had been one of the adults at the group home in Texas, where I'd been sent after my grandmother died. I still cringed at the memory of his sweaty hands. When he'd started backing me into corners and trying to touch me, I'd run away. I came here to Los Angeles. I'd always felt drawn here, and now I knew it had been because of Nate. We'd spent a lifetime dreaming about each other. We'd longed to be together before we even knew each other's name. Now we were together for real.

I stared out the bus window as we passed stores and houses. Why couldn't I relax? I loved Nate. He loved me. We were from different times but we'd still managed to be together. So why was I so sure that Sybil, or Gary, or *someone*, was going to pop up and destroy everything?

I hugged my backpack on my lap. 'Get a grip, Iris,' I told myself. 'You're both safe now.'

Two bus rides later, I was nearly home. The streets were shabby in this part of the city. Nate had told me that the whole area used to be farmland in 1922. Now it was concrete, with graffiti sprayed across the walls.

I sighed as I remembered the look on Nate's face when he'd first seen the place in this time. "It's not like this everywhere," I'd told him. I hated these ugly streets, too, but I still felt like I had to defend my time. "Some places are really pretty."

"Just not any place we can afford," Nate had said. Then he'd put his arms around me like he wished he hadn't said anything. "It's all right," he said. "There are plenty of awful places in my time, too."

I shook my head to clear the memory as I reached our building and opened the front door. Inside it was dark and smelled like a toilet. Our apartment was right at the very top. I trudged up the four dark flights of stairs. A homeless person was asleep on one of the landings.

I fumbled for my keys and opened the door. Our apartment was tiny – just one room and a kitchen. We had tried to make it as nice as we could. We'd painted the walls and bought pictures from a charity store. It should have felt like home, just because Nate and I lived there.

And it did, a bit. But ... I swallowed as I put down my bag. The truth was, ever since I'd been to Nate's time, I'd felt out of place in my own. I pushed the thought away as fast as I could.

Nate wasn't home yet. I went into the kitchen. When I turned on the light, some roaches scurried out of view. I shuddered. We kept everything clean, but the whole building was infested.

I started boiling water for pasta. We'd eaten the same thing for the last two nights, but it was all we had and it was cheap. We were lucky to have an apartment at all. Most places wanted you to pay a deposit when you first moved in, but the landlady here had felt sorry for us.

I stared down at the pot as the water started to bubble. I wished I knew how to cook. I wished my feet didn't hurt. Most of all, I wished that I didn't feel so strange and out of place here now. It was as if I could never relax. I remembered Nate's house in 1922 – how peaceful and cosy it had felt.

How had his family felt when he never came home?

I bit my lip as I thought for the millionth time of the panicked moment when I'd put the two halves of the stone together. There had been two ways they could fit. I hadn't known which was which – I just snapped the halves into place.

14

The stone had brought us here, to my time. Now it was locked solid.

Why, *why* hadn't I tried the other way?

There was the sound of a key in the lock. Relief filled me as Nate came in, closed the door behind him and hung up his charity-store jacket.

"Hi," he said.

I smiled. He looked so big and blond and solid. "Hi," I said back.

Nate seemed tired, but he came into the kitchen and wrapped his arms around me from behind. "You smell good," he whispered into my dark hair.

I turned and hugged him. Even after two months together, I still hadn't gotten used to how wonderful it felt to be able to touch each other. He wasn't just a dream any more – he was flesh and blood.

"I smell," I told him, "like a greasy diner."

Nate grinned. "Is that what it is? You should bottle it, like perfume."

I put my arms around his neck and we kissed. He'd been working as a labourer for these past two months, and his muscles were hard and strong. As the kiss grew deeper I felt dizzy. I rubbed my hands over his broad back and slipped them under his T-shirt. His skin was smooth and warm.

I wanted to do more than just kiss – a lot more. But I felt Nate shiver, and he pulled away. He swallowed and closed his eyes hard.

"I better go take a shower," he said at last. "I'm, um ... pretty dirty."

'Great, I'll take one with you,' I wanted to say. But I bit the words back.

Longing filled me as he left the room. I sighed and dumped the pasta in the pot. I listened to Nate take a shower, and tried not to picture him with the hot water pouring down over his bare skin. My fingers gripped the spoon. Maybe I sometimes felt like I was in the wrong time, but not when it came to the thought of me and Nate together. Then I was definitely a 21st-century girl.

What made it worse was that I knew Nate wanted me as much as I wanted him.

I looked over at the sofa. It unfolded into a bed at night. It was wonderful to lie in Nate's arms ... but it was also so frustrating I could die. On the first night we'd been here, Nate and I had lain in bed together – kissing each other – touching each other. It was like we were both on fire as we tugged each other's clothes off. Nate's body against mine was the most wonderful thing I'd ever felt.

I was just starting to think about the condoms I'd bought when Nate pulled away. "We can't," he gasped.

I was surprised – hurt. "Don't you want to?" I asked.

Nate touched my face. "Oh, I want to," he said in a low voice. "Iris, I want to so much. But ... I think we should wait until we're married."

I went very still. "Married?" I said at last.

Nate ran his thumb down my cheek and gave a small smile. "Oh, hell – that's not how I meant to ask you," he said. "But Iris, you *will* marry me, won't you?"

I gripped his hand hard. "Of course I will," I said. I didn't even have to think about it. There was no one for me but Nate – ever. "But we're not old enough yet," I said. Not without our parents' permission, anyway, which would be pretty tough in our case.

"The second we are, then," said Nate.

I nodded, my heart too full to speak. But my 18th birthday was still over a year away. I hesitated as I stroked Nate's firm arm. "Are you really saying you want to wait until then before we ...?"

Nate flopped on to his back and stared at the ceiling. "No," he said. "I don't *want* to wait at all. But ..." He shrugged, his cheeks a little red. "Well, in my time, that's what you do when you love a girl. You wait until you're married to her."

"But that's not what it's like in this time," I said softly. I kissed his shoulder. "I mean, people still wait sometimes, but no one thinks anything bad about you if you don't."

"I know," Nate said. His cheeks reddened even more. He'd seen enough TV shows by then to know I was right. He rolled over and rubbed my arm. His hand was warm and gentle as it slid up and down my skin. "I'm sorry," he said at last. "I know it's old-fashioned. I just … really want to be married to you before we do this."

I pressed close to him so that I could feel the thud of his heart under my hand – the softness of his chest hairs. "Don't be sorry," I said at last. "We'll wait."

I'd thought that I meant what I said. I *did* mean it. But it was so frustrating sometimes, especially with all our other worries – all the things that we never said out loud to each other.

It was as if the fact I couldn't really give myself to Nate made everything else loom even larger.

✑3✑

We had a small folding table that we ate on. I set it up and switched on the TV. It was about twenty years old, big and boxy. But I knew it was still like something out of science fiction to Nate.

Nate came out from the bathroom wearing a pair of jeans. His sandy hair was damp, and his muscles flexed as he pulled on a T-shirt. Nate looked great in modern clothes. When we went out together, other girls always checked him out. But I felt a pang any time I remembered the boy who'd looked almost ... formal in his tan trousers and white button-down shirt.

I opened my mouth to tell Nate that I missed his 1920s clothes, and then I stopped. I had clothes from 1922, too – Nate's mother had given them to me. And it was best to avoid any subject that touched on Nate's family.

Instead, we told each other about our days as we ate. Nate looked more tired than ever as he rubbed the stubble on his jaw. "The boss says we're right on time with this building," he said. "I only have another few weeks left there, I guess."

I winced. There was no way we could survive on what I made from the diner. "Can you get something else after that?" I asked.

Nate shrugged. "Maybe. The boss likes me. He says I'm a hard worker."

I knew that Nate didn't like the work much – it was just something he could get on the sly, without any I.D. The problem was that in this time, he didn't even exist. At some point, we'd have to go to the public records office and tell them some kind of story – maybe that all his records had been lost in a fire, or something. If we didn't he would never even be able to get a bank account, much less get married. But we'd decided to wait until I was 18, so social services couldn't take me in if someone realised I'd run away.

Nate's head was slumped on his hand as he picked at his meal. "You know what I'd really like to do?" he said.

I shook my head.

"I'd like to design buildings – not be the one to build them," he said.

My eyebrows shot up. "You mean you want to be an architect?"

Nate nodded. "Funny, isn't it?" he said. "Dad was always nagging me to figure out what I wanted to do. And now that I have, I can't do anything about it."

I started to protest that he *would* be able to … but then I fell silent. You have to make good grades to be an architect. Nate didn't have any grades at all – he'd never even been to school in this time. And even if he did, how could we ever afford for him to go to college?

I tried to smile. "Well, I never wanted to be a waitress, either, you know," I said. "Hey, maybe you could design a restaurant for us and we could run it together."

Nate smiled too. I could tell he felt bad about saying anything. "Great idea," he said. "We'll call it the Roaring Twenties Diner. People will come from miles around."

Then his mouth twisted and he looked down. I knew he was thinking about his family. I reached over and squeezed his hand hard, and he looked up and gave me a small smile.

"Sorry," he said.

"Don't be!"

"But I am," he said. "You can't look back. It doesn't do any good." He tugged at my hand. "Come on," he said. "Let's just ... not think for a while."

We moved to the sofa and curled up together. I stared at the TV screen as some stupid sitcom played. I could still feel Nate's sadness and I hurt for him.

When I'd been in Nate's time, Nate had never existed. The evil spirit Sybil had made sure of that, to keep Nate and me apart. His parents had been so sad. It was as if they were haunted by the son they'd never had. Then Nate and I had fixed what Sybil had done. Nate had existed again.

But then he'd had to leave his family for ever when the stone brought us to my time instead of his.

He hadn't even had a chance to say goodbye. Neither had I. I hadn't known his mother and little sister for very long, but I'd felt so close to both of them. It had hurt to leave them like that.

I swallowed as I looked over at my backpack in the corner. Nate and I had met in an old house up in the hills – a place in between times. When we'd left the house that first morning in this time, my backpack had been lying on the grass.

I should have been happy. There were things in it that I wouldn't want to lose. But, instead, it felt as if we'd been shut out from the 1920s. And that felt wrong. So wrong.

Nate tensed beside me as a show about World War Two came on. I reached for the remote control.

"No, leave it," Nate said. He sat up a little, gazing at the TV. I could see the tension in his jaw. A bomb went off on the screen.

It had been hard for Nate when he found out everything that had happened since his time. World War Two. The Korean War. Vietnam. Iraq. It must have seemed to him as if the world had gone crazy.

We watched the show in silence. Nate tapped his fist against his thigh. I knew he was wondering how many of his friends had been in the war. How many had never come home again.

When the show was over, he looked at me. His voice was hesitant.

"Do you ever think about your mother?" he asked.

It was the last question I was expecting. I went stiff. "No, I don't," I said.

Nate's sandy hair fell across his forehead. He played with the hem of his T-shirt. "Is she still in Texas?" he asked.

"I guess," I snapped. "Do we have to talk about her?"

Nate touched my arm. "Don't be angry. It's just that she's your only living relative. I thought …" He trailed off and looked embarrassed. "Never mind," he muttered.

All of a sudden I understood. Nate had lost his own family. Maybe he hoped that my mother would take us in and be like a family to us, too.

"Forget it, Nate," I said. "My mother lives on the streets. She's a drug addict – she abandoned me after my gran died." Then a thought crossed my mind. "Did you have drug addicts in the 1920s?"

Nate winced. "Yes," he said. "We called them dope fiends. I read that some of the Hollywood stars were addicted to morphine." He put his arms around me and I nestled close. "Oh, hell, Iris, I'm sorry," he murmured.

I stroked his arm. "Morphine is like heroin," I said. "That's what my mother's addicted to. So we're totally on our own, Nate. When we get married, she's not going to be there throwing flower petals."

Nate rested his cheek against my hair. "It doesn't matter," he said. "We're all that we need."

Yet I knew how much he missed his own family – how guilty and sad he felt about what they must have gone through when he disappeared. I shouldn't have said anything. I almost didn't.

But I cleared my throat and the words came out. "Nate, listen ... I've been going to the library to use the internet. I've been trying to find out what happened to your family. I need to know, too."

❦ 4 ❧

"Wake up, Iris. You have to take your pills."

The voice is insistent. I open my eyes. There's a nurse standing beside my bed. I sit up and squint in confusion at the sunshine coming in the window. It's late afternoon.

Then I remember – I'm in the mental ward of the hospital. There's no way out. No way to get word to Nate ... if he still wants to have anything to do with me. After Mel told me about the voices in her head, I'd felt so depressed that I'd come to my bedroom to lie down. I must have fallen asleep.

"I don't need any drugs," I tell the nurse.

"That's what you all say," she snaps. "Now, don't argue." She holds out two yellow pills. She's a big woman and she towers over me. She looks as if she'll stand there all day if I don't do what she says.

I hesitate, and then take the pills. I put them in my mouth and take a sip of water from the plastic cup she gives me. But I hold the pills under my tongue and don't swallow them.

I hand the cup back. "Good girl," the nurse says. "Time for your group therapy session now."

I swing my legs off the bed. "I just need to use the bathroom first," I tell her. I try not to mumble with the pills under my tongue. When I go into the bathroom I lock myself in one of the stalls and spit the pills in the toilet. My mouth tastes bitter. I flush the toilet and watch the pills swirl away.

Mel's in the bathroom too when I come out. I wash my hands at the sink and try not to look at her.

But she's staring right at me. I can't avoid her.

"It's true, isn't it?" she says. I think again how her sharp face makes her look like a stray cat.

"What is?" I say. But I know.

She leans close. "If you don't get back to the right time soon, you're going to die," she whispers into my ear.

I go cold with fear. She said before that I'm going to die soon, but I told myself she was just ranting like a crazy person. But *this* ... how can she know that I'm in the wrong time?

'I'm not,' I remind myself in a daze. 'Nate's the one who's out of place.' But then I think about what I found out at the library. And about the postcard from Gran that's still in my pocket – how faint its letters look now.

All of a sudden I'm terrified that Mel might be right. "What – what do you mean?" I stammer.

Mel leans against the sink and crosses her legs at the ankles. For a second it's like we're two girls in high school sharing gossip. But what she says next shatters that idea.

"See, the voices in my head told me all about it," she says.

"The ... voices?" I repeat.

She nods and taps her head above her ear. "I have a radio in my head," she says. She sounds so matter-of-fact. "It's on all the time. I think the aliens put it there."

I bite my lip. OK, so she *is* crazy. But still, she somehow knows something. "Mel, when you said I was in the wrong time ..." I start, and then I break off as the bathroom door swings open.

The nurse stands there. "Iris, come on, you're going to be late," she says. "You too, Mel."

Mel's face has gone blank. She walks out of the bathroom like she's in a dream.

Group therapy turns out to be a circle of chairs in one of the ugly green and brown rooms where we all sit. Dr Price asks us questions and we're supposed to share our feelings. Mel just gazes at her lap and giggles, as if the radio in her head is telling her funny things.

"Iris, welcome," Dr Price says. "Would you tell everyone a bit about yourself?"

I think of the postcard and almost laugh as I imagine telling the truth. But the idea that won't leave my head sounds too crazy even for this place. Besides, I have to convince them to let me out of here.

"Um, hi," I say. I give a little wave. "I'm Iris."

No one seems interested. I take a breath. "I was really confused last night," I say to the doctor. "But I feel much better now."

"I'm glad to hear it," he says. "Do you feel well enough to give me that object we were talking about?"

He means the stone. It's in my jeans pocket right now. I resist the urge to clutch it in my fingers. "No," I blurt out. "You see … well, it's from my dad. It means a lot to me."

"I see," Dr Price says. "OK, just checking."

I can tell he's not fooled. He knows I still believe that the stone is the only way Nate and I can be in the same time together – and to him, that means I'm nuts. He moves on.

"I want you all to think today about *responsibility*," he says to the whole group. "How can you best take responsibility for your own illnesses? Any ideas, gang?"

He actually says 'gang', as if we're all in a kids' TV show together. A boy holds back a snicker. When I glance over, he rolls his eyes. It seems I'm not the only one who hates it here.

A sudden chill touches me.

Maybe not, but I'm probably the only one who will die if I don't get out soon.

❦ 5 ❦

I spend the rest of the day wandering around the ward. I try to look innocent but I'm still searching for a way out. At some point, they *have* to make a mistake. Maybe I can slip away then. But they keep the door locked and there's always a guard.

I touch the stone in my pocket again. Then I notice something. I take out the stone and study it. It has green and silver swirls, joined together. The join has always been smooth … yet now there's a faint crack. My blood goes cold. What does this mean? It's almost as scary as the thing happening with the writing on the postcard.

I shove the stone back in my pocket. Before I can think, I go up to the nurse at the desk.

"Please," I say in a low voice. "I don't belong here. I have to get out."

She just glances at me and then checks a chart. "Iris Doe, right?" she says.

My last name isn't 'Doe', it's 'Morgan'. But I refused to tell them that, so they call me 'Doe'.

The nurse hums as she studies my chart. I grit my teeth. "Didn't you hear me?" I ask. "I have *got* to get out of here! I could die if I don't!"

She smiles and puts the chart away. "I think you're due for some more pills, Iris," she tells me. "You'll feel much better soon."

So then I have to go through the whole thing of hiding the yellow pills under my tongue again. I spit them out into a potted plant when no one's looking. Then I go back to my room and lie down. Mel isn't there, and I'm glad. I stare at the ceiling and hug myself. What does that crack in the stone mean?

Are Nate and I coming apart?

As I recall his last words to me – how angry he was – I wince. 'Nate, I'm so sorry,' I think. 'What happened is my fault.'

In my heart, I had known all along that Nate wouldn't want me to find out what happened to his family. We'd talked about it when we first arrived in this time. No one had even dreamed of the internet in 1922, but Nate had grasped it as soon as I explained it to him.

"There are birth records online, and –" I stopped short. I'd been about to say 'death records'. "Newspaper articles," I said instead. "We could find out what happened to your family, and then we'd *know*."

"No," he'd said. "I don't want to know. What if it's something terrible?" We'd gone to a garage sale that day, to buy clothes with the tiny bit of money I had so that we didn't stand out a mile. Nate pulled me behind a rack of clothes and gripped my hands. His brown eyes were intent.

"Iris, I'm here in *this* time now," he said. "I can't keep thinking about the past – I'll go screwy. I already feel like –" He stopped.

"What?" I said, worried.

He sighed and stroked his thumb across my fingers. "Your time is so strange," he said at last. "In some ways it's similar to mine, but – it's like things move a million times faster. I'm trying to belong here. But to do that, I've got to focus on the present. Just ... leave it, all right? My family. Please?"

"All right," I'd said at last.

I'd thought I meant it. Just like when I said I could wait till we were married,

But somehow ... somehow, I'd started going to the library to use their free computers. Every time I typed the names of Nate's family into the search engine, I told myself I was doing it for Nate, too. He was so sad all the time – I could see it in his eyes. It would help him to know what had happened.

Frederick Baxter. Grace Baxter. Ruth Baxter. I guessed at birth dates and entered everything I knew about them. But 'Baxter' was a common name. It took me weeks just to find out that his parents had gotten divorced in 1924. I'd stared at the screen in shock and then shut the window as fast as I could.

That's when I should have stopped searching. Divorce was unusual in 1924. It couldn't mean anything good.

But I kept on.

I lie on my bed in the hospital and think about the night I told Nate I'd been looking. The moment I'd said it, I'd wished I hadn't. He'd just sat on the sofa and stared at me. When he spoke, his voice was too quiet.

"What have you found out?" he asked.

"Nothing," I lied. The guilt of knowing what I did about his parents burned inside of me. Nate would be devastated if he knew.

He tapped his fist on the sofa and stared at the TV. "Don't look again," he said at last. "Please, Iris."

I bit my lip. I hated it that I knew something Nate didn't ... but I couldn't promise him anything. Nate shot me a look when I didn't speak. His dark eyes were troubled – angry.

"You're making it ten times harder for me to be here, you know," he said in a low voice.

I winced. "All right," I said. "I won't look again. I promise."

We didn't speak the rest of that night. We made up the sofa bed and for the first time, we didn't sleep in each other's arms. I lay and hugged myself, so aware of Nate next to me. I wanted to nestle up beside him, but I was afraid he'd turn away. I knew him as well as I knew myself. When Nate was angry he detached himself from others.

And he was right to be angry. It was *his* family, not mine. I didn't have any business poking around in their history if he didn't want me to.

But the next day, I went back to the library.

Nate had found me there.

Oh God, the things he had said ... it felt as if it could really be the end of us. Yet the things I'd found out that day were even worse.

I roll over on the hospital bed and take the postcard from Gran out of my jeans pocket. I'm not surprised to see that her writing is fainter than ever.

I'm running out of time. I know it.

I start as Mel comes in. She doesn't look at me as she lies down on her bed.

"Mel?" I say.

No answer.

I go over to her bed. I sit down beside her and show her the postcard. I pull out the stone and show her that, too. "Mel, look," I say. "You know something about these things, I know you do! Tell me what you know. *Please.*"

She sits up. She takes the stone from me and turns it over in her hands. She frowns as if she's thinking. I hold my breath.

Then she giggles and starts to sing:

"Some sunny day with a smile on my face
I'll go back to that place far away.
Oh, how I pine for those lips sweet as wine
Pressed close to mine, some sunny day."

The song has a happy tune, for all the words are so sad. Why does it sound familiar? Then I freeze as I remember. It's from Nate's time. I heard it on the big wooden radio at his house.

Why is Mel singing a song from 1922? How on earth does she know it?

She's finished now. She traces the faint crack in the green and silver stone with her fingers.

"Running out of time," she murmurs.

"What do you mean?" I snap. "Mel! Tell me!"

She laughs and gives me back the stone. "Just like Dorothy," she says. She wiggles her fingers in my face like she's pretending to be a witch. "Where's your hourglass, Dorothy?" she teases. "Is the wicked witch still after you?"

I try for a long time, but can't get anything out of her that makes sense. At last I go back to my own bed and huddle under the covers. What did Mel mean? The only wicked witch who was after Nate and me was Sybil. And Sybil is dead now.

But everything seems to be falling apart anyway.

⊙6⊙

Dr Price taps a pen on his desk as he watches me. Neither of us has spoken for several minutes. I slump in my chair. I didn't sleep last night. Maybe it would help if I took the pills they keep shoving at me, but there's no way I'm swallowing that stuff.

"One of the nurses tells me that you spoke to her at the front desk yesterday," Dr Price says at last.

I shrug.

"She says you told her that you don't belong here, and that you could die if you don't get out. What did you mean by that?" he asks.

Damn. I should have known that nothing I said here would be private. When I still don't say anything, the doctor sighs. "Iris ... we're trying to help you," he says.

And I know he *is* trying. It's just that he's so totally wrong that it's a joke.

He refuses to give up, I'll say that much for him. "Do you feel that you're in danger here?" he asks. "Are you scared of something?"

I rub my head. I know there's no point in telling him ... but then again, I don't have much to lose. There's no way out of this place – I've been trying to find one for two days now. And I can't trick him into believing I'm sane when he knows about the stone.

"I just have to leave," I say. "I shouldn't be here. I can't tell you why because you'll think I'm crazy. But I'm not."

"We don't use the word 'crazy' here," Dr Price says in a kind voice.

"Well, whatever word you use, then," I say. "I'm totally sane, all right?"

He smiles a little. "I'm not sure anyone is *completely* sane," he says. "Not me, not you. But I do think you have some problems, Iris."

He has no idea how right he is. I want to bring out the postcard and shove it under his nose – show him how faint the letters are now. But he wouldn't understand. He'd just write it all down in my notes.

My fists are tight. Even if I got out of here, how could I fix everything that's gone wrong?

Dr Price talks on for a long time. He tells me that he knows how hard it is to be 'ill'. But if I just keep taking my pills and talk to him, if I trust him and the other doctors, then everything will be fine.

I stop listening to him. Instead, I think about that terrible day in the library.

I'd just worked for ten hours straight at the diner, yet I'd still stopped to search the internet before I went home. I felt guilty as I walked into the library. I knew I shouldn't be there, not after I'd promised Nate … but I couldn't help myself. I had to know the truth, even if it was just for me.

I looked up the story in the 1924 newspaper about Nate's parents' divorce and I read it again. It was only a few lines long. It hardly told me anything – just the bare facts.

I stared at the screen. What had happened?

Nate wouldn't talk about his family much any more. But from what he'd said, his parents had been happy. For them to get a divorce in 1924 – a time when it was so rare to do that – things must have become awful between them.

I felt sick. Somehow I knew it was because Nate had disappeared. His family had been so close. It must have torn them apart when he just vanished one day and never came back.

Tears came into my eyes as I thought of Ruth. She was Nate's little sister – and I felt as if she were mine, too. She'd tried so hard to help me find Nate when I'd been trapped in his time without him.

For weeks now, I'd tried to discover what had happened to her. I knew Nate's parents had to be dead – almost a hundred years had passed since 1922. But Ruth might not be.

The noise of the library seemed to fade as I gazed at the flashing cursor. Just like Nate had hoped we might find my mother, I guess I hoped the same thing about Ruth. It wasn't impossible. She'd be very old, but she might still be alive. She might have a family of her own who could help us.

I bit my lip as a feeling of dread came over me. By now, I'd tried almost all the search terms I could think of to find Ruth. But there was one word I hadn't tried. I hadn't even wanted to think about it.

Very slowly, I typed, 'Ruth Margaret Baxter death'.

It took a moment to make myself hit 'Enter'. 'I won't find anything,' I told myself. 'The name's too common. Besides, she probably got married and her name won't be Baxter anyway.'

The thought gave me hope. I clicked the mouse.

Thousands of hits came up. As I scrolled down the pages, I started to relax. None of these

Ruth Baxters were the right ones. But then
I saw the headline – 'Woman Found Dead by
Neighbours'.

And I knew it had to be Ruth.

I felt numb as I clicked on the story. It was
from a 1971 newspaper. 'Ruth Baxter, 61, was
found dead in her apartment today ...'

There was a photo of the woman. It was the
right Ruth – I recognised her dark eyes. Tears
came to my own eyes again as I read. 'She
always seemed so sad,' a neighbour said. 'She
told us that she hadn't been happy since a family
tragedy when she was 12 years old.'

A family tragedy when she was 12 years old.
That was when Nate had disappeared.

I bumped my fist against my mouth. She was
still called Ruth *Baxter*. So she'd never married.
And she'd lived on her own. The story said
she'd died from an overdose. They weren't sure
whether it was suicide. There'd been no note.
But then, it sounded as if she hadn't had anyone
to leave a note for.

She'd been all alone.

The words seemed to swim in front of me. I hadn't known it was possible to feel so sad. Ruth – the bright, chattering girl who had seemed wise beyond her years. This is what had happened to her.

'No,' I thought in a daze. 'It wasn't supposed to be like this.' The second I thought it, I knew it was true. This was more than just a sad story about someone I cared for. It was *wrong*.

As wrong as I felt in my own time, now.

"Iris?"

I spun around in my seat. Nate stood behind me. My cheeks went hot. In a rush, I closed the window on the screen and jumped up. "Nate! What are you doing here?"

I thought again how big and solid he looked, with his sandy hair and strong features. He hesitated. "I felt bad about last night," he said. "I thought I'd walk you home from the diner, but they told me you'd already left. I had a feeling I'd find you here."

"I'm sorry," I said. We kept our voices low, but people still looked over at us. "Nate, I know I said that I wouldn't look any more. But ..." I trailed off.

There was concern in Nate's eyes as he looked at me ... along with something almost like fear. He started to touch my hand, then let his fingers fall away.

"What have you found out?" he asked in a flat tone.

I couldn't answer.

He sat down in the chair and put his hand on the mouse.

"Nate, no!" I cried. "Please don't!"

It only took him a second to figure out the 'Back' button. Before I could stop him, the story about Ruth came up on the screen again.

He read it in silence. I sank down into an empty chair beside him. Why had I had to keep looking? Why couldn't I have left it alone the way he'd asked me to?

The look on his face tore at my heart. "Nate?" I whispered.

He didn't reply. He read the story, and then he hit 'Back' again and again. Soon the story about his parents' divorce appeared. He read that without speaking, too.

I squeezed his hand. "Please say something," I begged.

He looked at me then and his eyes were bright. "Don't," he said.

It felt as if he'd slapped me. I pulled away. "Don't what?" I said.

"Just ... don't talk to me."

I loved him so much that it hurt. "Nate, listen," I said. "This is all wrong! What happened to Ruth, and your parents – it wasn't how things were supposed to be, I'm sure of it!"

His brown eyes flashed. "Is that supposed to help?" he said. "It *is* what happened! It's all in the past now – we can't change it!"

I started to answer, and then stopped. He was right.

Nate gripped my arms. "Don't you think I knew how terrible it would be for them?" he demanded. "That's why I didn't want to know what happened to them! But now I know. I can never *un*-know. And it's even worse than I thought!"

I struggled to get the words out. "I'm sorry," I said. "I'd never have told you."

The chair scraped as Nate stood up. "Yeah," he said. He sounded bitter. "Just like you never told me about the Great Depression, or World War Two, or Vietnam, or –"

"Nate, you know what it was like when we first met at the old house!" I cried. "Why would I talk about those things?" We'd been too busy talking about ourselves – each other. Too busy falling in love even more deeply than we'd already been.

Nate was breathing hard. He ran a hand over his face as if he were struggling for control.

"Yes, I remember," he said. When he dropped his hand, I shrank at the look in his eyes.

"And you know what, Iris?" he said in a low voice. "I wish to hell that I'd never even gone into that old house. It would have been better if you'd just stayed a dream."

I stood frozen – stunned. For a second I thought I saw regret in Nate's eyes, then his jaw tightened and he walked away.

Part of me wanted to go after him. Part of me never wanted to see him again. I ducked my head against the curious looks from the library users around me, and wondered at the pain of being so hurt by someone I loved so much.

But then … I'd hurt Nate, too. Not on purpose, but I had. He'd have to live with all he knew about his family for the rest of his life now. He'd never be able to forget it.

Had he meant what he'd said? Did he really wish that we'd never met?

All of a sudden I wanted my gran, more than I'd ever wanted anyone. I swallowed hard and sat down at the computer again. I typed her name into the search engine – Helen Josephine Morgan.

Just as I'd hoped, a story from a Texas newspaper came up about when she'd died. I didn't want to read about that – I just wanted to see her photo. I sat holding my elbows as I drank in her face. As I remembered how much she'd loved me, I began to feel a little better.

"I miss you, Gran," I whispered.

Then I glanced at the story, and I couldn't hold back a gasp. I stared at the screen. The room seemed to spin around me.

I'd never known Gran's maiden name until now ... but there it was, in black and white.

It was 'Baxter'.

❧ 7 ❧

"Iris?" says Dr Price.

All of a sudden I realise that I've been sitting here not listening to him for a long time. I look up.

"You seem deep in thought," he says. "Is there anything you'd like to tell me?"

I just shrug. There is no way I can tell him what I'm thinking about.

That day in the library, I'd spent hours at the computer, frantic as I searched for details about my grandmother. At last I'd found a story from a 1932 newspaper that took my breath away.

The headline read, 'Baby Saved from Burning Car'.

The story told how a newborn baby girl named Helen had been rescued from the car crash and fire that killed her parents. And the couple who'd saved her were Iris and Nathaniel Baxter.

Iris and Nathaniel.

Oh, my God. I'd gaped at the screen – at my name beside Nate's. "We don't have children of our own yet," the Iris in the story had said. "My husband and I hope very much that we can adopt Helen."

It felt like the world was spinning around me all over again. The story showed a photo of a woman holding a baby, with a man standing behind her. I gasped out loud, as if I'd been punched. The photo was grainy black and white, but it was me and Nate.

My fingers had felt numb as I checked adoption records. There it was … Helen Josephine, adopted by Iris and Nathaniel Baxter in 1932.

Our adopted daughter. Mine and Nate's. Could it be true?

I had one thing of Gran's with me in my backpack – a postcard she had sent me when she went to Dallas for some medical tests. I dug it out and turned it over. I knew what it said, of course – 'Dear Iris, Everything's fine but I miss my girl! Home soon. Love, Gran.'

This time, my scalp prickled as I read it. I'd had it for years, and the ink from the biro she had used had always looked fresh. Now the message was fading ... as if Gran herself was fading out of history.

And when I stared back at the adoption record on the computer screen, I had a terrible feeling that I knew why. I saw again that moment when I'd snapped the stone together. There'd been no time to work out how its two halves fitted – I'd just chosen a way.

My choice had been more wrong than I could ever have imagined.

Back in the present, Dr Price watches me from across the desk. "Iris?" he says again.

I shake my head. "No, there's nothing I want to tell you," I say. I can just imagine how well it would go if I did. 'Guess what,' I might say. 'I'm in the wrong time, just like I thought! Because it turns out that my grandmother is supposed to be my adopted daughter. And if Nate and I aren't in the past to save her from a burning car, then soon *I* won't exist, either, because Gran won't have had my mother to give birth to me!"

Somehow I don't think this would convince him that I'm sane.

I'd left the library that day in a daze. Everything felt far too weird and unreal. I went home, but Nate hadn't been there. Hours passed. At last, when it was dark, I went out looking for him. I'd wandered for hours, scared, wanting him so badly. I needed to tell him I was sorry. Nothing was the way it was supposed to be and it was all my fault. We *had* to find a way to get back to the 1920s.

I knew the stone was the key ... but if I tried to break it, what if that made things worse? Finally I'd sunk down on to a park bench, too tired to cry. A woman passed by. When she saw me she came back.

"Are you OK?" she asked.

She sat down beside me – and I'd been so upset that I just told her what was wrong. She was a good listener … or at least, I thought she was.

It turned out that she was a police officer. And she thought I was either on drugs or crazy. That's how I ended up here. And now time's running out, and there's nothing I can do about it.

The silence in the room feels heavy. Dr Price watches me as if he thinks I'll speak if he just waits long enough. I don't.

"All right, Iris, you can go now," he says at last.

I get up and leave.

I'm not sure how, but I survive the rest of the day. I sit in silence in group therapy. Later I stare at the TV set with the others. And always, always, I keep an eye on the front door.

But I'm starting to lose hope now. When I take out the postcard again, my hand shakes. The letters are hard to see. It seems as if every minute that passes sees our chances of getting back to the 1920s grow smaller and smaller.

What will happen when the writing is gone?

I swallow hard and put the postcard away. I want Nate so badly – but what he said was true, whether he meant it or not. It *would* have been better if we'd stayed a dream to each other. Then no one would have got hurt. His parents might have had a long and happy marriage. Ruth's entire life might have been different.

The TV blurs as tears fill my eyes. I swipe them away, angry with myself. Nate and I are soul mates ... but I guess even with soul mates, the price is sometimes just too high.

How can you be happy when you know you've brought such sadness to others?

"Trick or treat," a voice whispers.

I jump and look up. Mel is sitting beside me again. Her eyes aren't dull now – they're alive with interest.

"Trick or treat," she repeats.

I don't have time for Mel. Maybe I'd thought she could help me at first, but now everything seems hopeless. I sigh and gaze at the ceiling. "I don't have a treat to give you," I say.

"Then I'll give you one," she says. "Let me see that stone again."

I hesitate, then take it out of my pocket. I hand it to her. No one pays any attention to us. They're all off in their own little worlds.

Mel strokes the place where the join is visible. "It's wrong," she says.

My heart skips. "What do you mean?"

"It's like a puzzle piece that's been forced to fit," she says. "Nothing will ever be right for either of you while it's *this* way."

She hands the stone back and I grip it hard. She said 'either of you'. I've never mentioned

Nate to her ... but somehow she knows about him.

My voice shakes. "How do I get it back the right way?" I ask. She doesn't answer. I touch her arm. "Mel! Please tell me!"

She shrugs. "That's easy," she says. "You just have to want it."

The stone gleams with green and silver lights. Hope stirs in me. I touch the join and think, 'Please put Nate and me back in his time.' I will it to happen as strongly as I can. Please. Please. Please.

Nothing changes. Yet I know Mel is telling the truth. It's as if the radio in her head has a lot of static, but sometimes it can pick up something that's true. I cup the stone in both hands and try again, harder.

'Please, *please*,' I think. 'We *have* to get back to 1922. Mel's right. Nothing will ever be OK for us if we don't.'

But nothing happens. My heart sinks as the truth hits me. Of course I can't do it alone. The stone is me *and* Nate – it has two halves – pieces of both of our souls. I need him, too.

Mel's playing with something in her hand. It's a box of matches. I almost ask what she's doing with them – no one's allowed to smoke in here. Before I can, she leans in close and hisses, "Someone's coming for you, Iris. They're on their way right now."

I stare at her. "Who?"

She puts the matches in her pocket. "Someone you know," she says with a wide smile. Then she starts to hum. As I recognise the song, I freeze. It's 'Ding, Dong, the Witch is Dead'.

Just yesterday, I called Sybil 'the wicked witch' in my head. But Mel *can't* mean that Sybil's coming! Sybil is dead!

I grab her arm. "What are you trying to tell me?" I gasp. "Who's coming?"

Mel's face has gone blank again. She stares at the TV.

I panic. The fear that's been following me for two months slams into me, full force. Sybil, or *someone*, is going to appear and ruin everything for me and Nate for ever. If that happens before we can figure out the stone, then time will run out for me.

"Mel, you've got to tell me!" I cry.

She hums the same tune under her breath. 'Ding, Dong ...'

I jump to my feet, still holding the stone. "Tell me!" I shout at Mel. "Tell me who's coming!"

The guard rushes up, along with two male nurses. "Easy, easy!" one of the men cries. They grab me and pin my hands behind my back. The stone falls to the floor with a clatter.

"Let me go!" I yell. "You don't understand! Something evil is coming!" I kick and struggle, but there are three of them and they're too strong for me. Mel just sits there and gazes at the TV.

One of the nurses picks up the stone and shakes his head. "We'd better lock this away with the rest of her things," he says. "It's too dangerous when she's like this – she could knock someone over the head with it."

"No! No!" I shout. I'm crying now, thrashing about as hard as I can. "Give it back! I have to have it – time's running out!"

"Sorry, hon," one of the men says. "This is for your own good." The next thing I know, I feel a pinprick of pain in my hip.

Darkness swoops down over me and the world goes black.

8

When I wake up, I'm in my bed. The room is dark except for a small nightlight. Mel's asleep in the other bed – I can hear her breathing.

My arm throbs where one of the nurses twisted it. My head feels full of cotton wool from the shot they gave me. All I know is that I have to get out of here. I push back the covers.

The second I move, a nurse appears – the same big woman as before. "You're awake," she says. "Here, just in time for these." She holds out more pills and I shrink back.

"I don't need them," I tell her.

"Take them."

I want to argue, but my head hurts. I take the pills and put them under my tongue. I take a gulp of water and hand the cup back to her.

This time she just stands there. "Show me the inside of your mouth," she says.

I want to cry. There's no way out. I swallow the pills – they make me gag as they go down my dry throat.

I open my mouth and the nurse gives a grim smile. "It's easier when you take them with water," she says, and leaves the room. I hear her lock the door behind her.

I shiver and lie back down on the bed. What will the pills do to me?

I glance over at Mel. She seems so peaceful – but I know she's crazy, no matter what Dr Price wants to call it. Yet she's the one person who understands what's going on.

I feel shaken. I take out the postcard and study it in the dim light. Does the writing look fainter? Or is it the same? I can't tell.

Maybe all of them are right and I really *am* crazy. Maybe I've just invented all of this in my head.

"No," I whisper. "I didn't make it up. His name is Nate ... short for Nathaniel." I hug myself, wishing that it were Nate's arms around me. I've never felt so alone, not even after Gran died and I got sent to the group home.

'Nate, I need you,' I think as I stare into the darkness. 'I need you.'

At last I fall asleep.

"Can I please have my stone back?" I ask the nurse at the desk.

It's the next day. I've had breakfast and taken a shower. I should feel better, brighter. Instead it's a struggle to make my voice sound calm.

"No, I'm sorry," the nurse says. "Dr Price feels that it's making you too upset."

I grip the side of the desk. "I'm *upset* because I *don't have* it!"

She goes back to her paperwork. "You can talk to Dr Price about it later," she says.

"When?" I ask.

"When he's here."

"Yes, but *when*?" I cry.

She gives me a level look. "Iris ... calm down," she says. "He'll be here sometime in the afternoon."

I want to shout at her, but the guard's watching. They might grab me again and give me another shot. I'm shaking with fear and anger. I turn and go into the TV room. I sink on to the sofa and rub my arms.

What am I going to do? I have *got* to get that stone back, or I won't have any chance at all of fixing what's wrong.

If I live long enough to try, that is.

The hours drag past. I sit and stare at the TV without taking anything in. I probably look as hopeless as the other patients now.

At last I hear the buzzer, which means someone's at the main door. I glance up – and then realise how stupid it is to think I might escape. How can I go anywhere while they've got the stone?

I watch the door anyway. A tall boy a little older than me enters the common area, and I can't hold back a gasp. A nurse holds his arm. He's wearing jeans and a blue T-shirt – his sandy hair is rumpled.

It's Nate.

My heart hammers like a wild thing. As the nurse checks him in, his dark eyes find mine. Somehow I manage not to let my expression change. I don't want anyone in charge to realise that I know him – I don't know what they'd do if they did.

But as our eyes meet, I can see his relief that he's found me. My own relief is so great that it feels as if my bones have turned to water. I tear my glance away and stare at the TV. My thoughts pound in my head.

Why have they brought Nate here? How did he know where I was?

It seems like hours before we get a chance to talk. Nate's taken away to be given a bedroom. But at last he comes back to the common area and settles on a sofa near me. We don't look at each other.

My chest feels tight. I'm so aware of him, just a few feet away. But I remember what he said to me – 'It would have been better if you'd stayed a dream.' Oh God, did he mean it? Maybe I only imagined the look of relief on his face. Maybe he's not glad to see me at all.

An advert comes on the TV. Nate looks bored. He gets up and stretches and then he leaves the room and doesn't come back.

I look at the corridor he's vanished down. I feel tense – uncertain. Does he want me to follow him? Or does he hate me now?

I don't know. But I have to try.

After a few minutes I get up and leave the room, too. I try to look casual as I walk down the dorm hallway where Nate went. A door opens as I pass. "In here," a voice whispers.

As I turn, Nate pulls me into a tiny single bedroom and shuts the door. The next second his arms are around me and he's holding me as if he'll never let me go.

"I found you," he says in a choked voice. "Oh, God, I really found you –"

I let out a sob as we hug each other. His chest is warm against my cheek. "How – how did you know where I was?" I ask.

There are dark circles under Nate's eyes, and stubble on his jaw. "I've been looking for days," he says. "I've been going out of my mind. And then at last I found an old homeless guy who heard you talking to the woman on the park bench. He knew she was a cop. He guessed you'd been taken in."

Nate strokes my hair from my face. "It took me for ever to find out where they'd taken you," he says. "I knew I couldn't get you out. I just had to pretend I was crazy and hope they'd bring me here, too."

I'm crying, but I still have to laugh. "You pretended you were crazy on purpose? That really *is* crazy."

"I'd have done a hell of a lot more to get you back." He takes my face in his hands and kisses me. *Nate.* It feels as if I'm melting in sunshine. I press close against him, and kiss him back as hard as I can.

At last Nate pulls away and grips my hands. His eyes look tormented. "I'm sorry," he says. "Iris, I am so sorry. I didn't mean what I said. I was just so upset about my family – about Ruth –"

"I know," I break in. "It's OK."

"It's not OK!" He touches my face. "You're my life. You always have been. I can't help being sad about my family, but I'm happy with *you*. I love you."

"I love you too," I whisper. But then I think about how the join in the stone is uneven, and I have a terrible feeling that Mel is right. Nothing will ever be good for Nate and me in this time.

Nate rests his head against mine. "I'm sorry I ran off and left you," he says. "I just couldn't handle knowing what had happened to my family – knowing that it's all my fault –"

"It's not your fault!" I burst out. "It's mine – I put the stone together wrong!"

Nate gapes at me. "*What?* That wasn't your fault! It was just chance."

"Listen!" As fast as I can, I explain everything that's happened. The only thing I don't tell him is what Mel said yesterday – that someone is coming. All of this feels impossible enough already without adding *that* to it.

Nate stares down at the postcard when I show it to him. I feel cold with fear. The writing is almost invisible now. If you didn't know what the message said, you wouldn't be able to read it.

Nate's fingers are white as he clutches the card. He looks up at me. "She's ... she's really going to be our adopted daughter?" he whispers.

My throat is tight. "I think so," I say. "And time's running out for me. We've got to get back there somehow."

I see Nate's jaw harden. "We've got to hurry, then," he says. "We have *got* to get that stone back."

I nod. "It's somewhere behind the nurses' station, but we can't get in there – someone will see us!"

Nate grips my hand tight. "There's got to be a way!" he says. "Iris, it all makes sense now. We're meant to be in my time together – we always were!"

I know he's right ... but life doesn't always go the way it's supposed to. Then I pull my shoulders back. No – I refuse to think that way. I *will* have a happy life with Nate, or I will die trying.

"OK," I say in a rush. "Let's try to think –"

I freeze at the sound of steps in the hallway. Nate and I throw each other a startled glance. I steel myself for a nurse to come in and find us. Instead there's a light, tinkling laugh that makes my scalp prickle.

"Fire," a voice says.

∝ 9 ∞

Nate throws open the door. The voice was Mel's, but there's no sign of her now. We can see smoke curling down the hallway, and we hear shouts.

The fire alarm goes off. Its shrill bell wails through the air.

"Oh Christ, what has she done?" I gasp.

Nate and I run back to the main ward. I stop in my tracks, my eyes streaming with smoke. Screams fill the room. The curtains are on fire. They snap and crackle with flame. There's another fire on the sofa. A male nurse tries to beat it out with a pillow, and another nurse pulls him away.

"It's spreading too fast!" he shouts. "We've got to get everyone out! Go check the rooms!"

The air is dark with smoke now. A sprinkler system has come on, but it's not helping much.

"Remember our fire drills!" the guard shouts. "Form a line!" He throws open the main door. People ignore him and race for it in a stampede.

Nate grabs my hand. I know what he's thinking, because it's what I'm thinking, too. We dash for the nurses' station. The nurses have already gone. We run around to the far side, where the guard can't see us for smoke. Nate vaults over the desk and I clamber over, too.

There's a small office behind the desk. I run into it. The smoke isn't so bad here. I don't know where to look, but then I see a shelf. It's full of plastic trays with names on them. Mine says 'Iris Doe' – only 'Doe' has been crossed out and 'Morgan' written over it.

I stare. How did they find out my last name?

No time to think. Nate snatches the plastic tray down. My backpack isn't there, but everything that was in it is. The stone gleams up at me. Oh, thank God! I grab it. Dimly, I notice that Nate's taken something, too, and put it in his pocket.

"Hurry!" I say. I hold the stone out to him. "Maybe if we both touch it, and think about how much we need to be back in your time –"

Nate nods and grips the stone. Then all of a sudden he jerks away. "No!" he cries. "Iris, we're up on the seventh floor – I don't think this building even existed in my time!"

Horror fills me as I realise what he means. We could fall to our deaths if we went back to 1922 from here. "We've got to get to the ground!" I say.

"Come on!" Nate grabs my hand again and we leave the small office. The smoke is like a black wall. I cough and cover my mouth. Tears stream down my cheeks. I can hear the fire, like loud, crackling static, and wonder if this is what the inside of Mel's head sounds like.

We climb back over the desk again and head for the main door, stumbling through the smoke. "There you are!" a voice cries. It's one of the nurses. Sweat pours down his face. He grabs us and ushers us out the door.

"The fire engines are coming," he gasps as he bangs it shut. "You're the last two out. Go down the stairs – join the others in the parking lot at the fire meeting point."

We don't argue – we take off at a run. We duck into the stairwell and pound down the stairs. They turn around and around as we go lower and lower.

All of a sudden I feel so strange. Dizzy. I take the postcard out of my pocket as we run and almost pass out.

The writing is gone.

My heart pounds in horror. Then I look again and see it's still there – but so faint it's almost invisible. Another few minutes – that's all I have.

"Nate!" I cry in a panic.

He goes pale as he sees what the problem is. "No!" he gasps. "We can't let this happen!"

He grips my hand and we both run faster. We reach the ground floor and burst out the door. We're in the main lobby of the hospital now. The fire alarms are still going off. People look nervous, but they're not making anyone leave this floor yet. But there are too many people here to try anything with the stone – someone might stop us.

We sprint through the lobby. We race out the front doors. The others from our ward stand on the far side of the parking lot. Mel is a little apart from the others. She grins and makes a thumbs-up sign to us.

She started the fire on purpose, I realise in a daze. She was trying to help me and Nate!

Then I freeze. There's a man getting out of a car. His dark hair is slicked back like he thinks he's a movie star. There are two other social workers with him. He glances over and his eyes widen.

Then he smiles.

I see him say my name to the other two. They start over to us. Their stride is quick and confident. For a second the world seems to tilt.

Nate grips my arms. "Iris! What is it?"

"Gary," I whisper.

"Gary?"

"From the group home!" I shiver as I recall the feel of his sweaty hands on me. Mel had tried to warn me that someone bad was coming. The police must have found out who I am – that's how the hospital got my last name.

I come back to myself in a flash. I feel even dizzier now – weaker than ever. I don't need to look to know that the writing on the postcard is about to disappear for good.

"Nate, hurry!" I gasp. I hold the stone out to him. "We've got to do it *now*."

Nate's jaw is set rock hard. He glares over at Gary, and I know how much he wants to confront him. But he takes a deep breath and grips the stone.

"I love you," he says in a low voice. "It'll be all right."

We hold the stone together. Nate's fingers are warm against my own. I think as hard as

I can, 'Please take us back to 1922 – it's where we're meant to be – we *have* to get back there.'

At first nothing happens. Then the stone begins to hum. The faint crack grows larger. The two pieces are coming apart.

Nate's eyes meet mine. I know we're thinking the same thing. We can only share a time when the two parts of the stone are together. So when they come apart, we'll have to put them back the right way very fast.

But can we be fast enough? Or will we be separated for good?

I keep looking into Nate's eyes. My heart beats hard. I feel so dizzy now – so strange. Then I hear a moan and realise it's me. My knees sag. I stumble.

"What are you doing to her?" Gary shouts. He and the others start to run.

Nate grabs me in his arms as I fall. "Keep hold of the stone with me!" he cries. "Iris, you *cannot* die! I won't let you!"

I try to clutch the stone, but can feel the life slipping away from me. Oh God, we're too late! Then my heart leaps as the stone starts to come apart.

Yes!

All of a sudden Gary grabs me. "We're taking you home, Iris," he says.

"Let go of me!" I cry as he drags me away from Nate. I try to struggle but I'm so weak.

"Get your hands off her, you bastard!" Nate shouts. He lunges at Gary, but the other social workers grip his arms from behind.

"You're killing her!" he shouts at Gary. "Let us go!"

Gary's hands are sweaty on my arm and his breath is fast. It brings back terrible memories. I *cannot* let this creep ruin things. I grit my teeth and somehow rip free. With all my strength, I spin around and knee him in the groin, hard.

"You little bitch!" he gasps as he doubles over.

I try to reach Nate but one of the male nurses is there now, holding me back. "Easy, Iris!" he says.

"Let me go!" I cry. "You don't understand!"

Nate manages to pull away from the others. He lunges for me but they grab him again. His muscles strain beneath his T-shirt as he struggles.

He's still holding the stone. Our hands crane towards each other. My fingers touch the stone again. My gaze is locked with Nate's.

'Please, please!' I think.

With a green and silver flash, the stone comes apart.

And then ... everything changes.

I'm tumbling through space. Wind shrieks past me. I can see blurred images of other times, just like in the dreams Nate and I used to share. Is he there? I can't tell.

"Nate!" I scream. "*Nate!*"

Somewhere far off, I can hear him shouting too. Or am I just imagining it? I shove aside my fear and try to move towards the sound.

My heart jumps as I feel his hand. Our fingers clutch at each other, then the wind tears us apart. My hair lashes across my face as I gasp and struggle back to him.

"Iris!" Nate yells. He sounds both close and far away. Somehow our hands find each other again and our fingers grip tight. I feel something smooth in his palm.

His half of the stone! Acting as one, Nate and I fit the two pieces together again. There's a bright, blinding flash. I cry out as the wind rips us apart again and pummels me like a leaf in a storm, tumbling me over and over until I can't think any more.

Then darkness.

✺ 10 ✺

I wake up slowly. I feel so tired – but warm and safe, too. Part of me never wants to open my eyes. When I do, all I can see is a bright white light.

'Is this heaven?' I think in a daze. Maybe I've died after all.

Then I blink. The light is sunshine. A tree's branches are spread up above me, and its leaves are bright green in the sun. Nate's arms are around me. He's sitting against the tree, cradling me to his chest.

He strokes my hair away from my face. "Iris?" he whispers.

I wince as I sit up. I lick my lips and look around us. "Is this ...?" I start to say.

Nate nods. "We're back in 1922," he says in a soft voice. "I recognise these fields – it's where the hospital was in your time."

I let out a breath. I'm shaking and for a moment I can't speak. I lean forward and press myself against Nate's chest. His heart beats hard against mine as we hold each other tight.

I never want to let him go.

At last I look up again. I gaze around me at the green fields, and at the buildings of Los Angeles in the distance. There are no skyscrapers, no planes in the sky up above.

"We did it," I murmur.

Nate nods. "We did," he says.

He shows me the stone and I gasp. It's so beautiful now! It was always pretty, with its green and silver lights – but somehow it never looked right. Now it's perfect.

I touch it in awe. The join is invisible. I know that it will never come apart again.

Nate's sandy hair falls over his forehead as he studies the stone too. Then his hand closes over it. "I want you to know something," he says. My heart tightens as his dark eyes meet mine.

"If we'd had to stay in your time, we'd have made it work, somehow," he says. He touches my face. "I love you, Iris. That will never change, no matter what time we're in."

I reach up and hold his hand in mine. "I know," I say.

We both start to smile. All of a sudden we're grinning like fools. It feels like the sunshine is inside of me – inside both of us. Nate scoops me into his arms again and we fall, laughing, to the soft, grassy ground.

Hours later, we're walking along a road high up in the hills. The sun beats down. It's the same road that I found the day Nate and I first met. All I knew then was that I felt drawn to come here – and that I was haunted by a boy who lived in my dreams.

I start to say something, then stop in my tracks. The postcard! I grab it from my jeans pocket. My jaw drops.

It's still the same, but the image looks brand new. The other side is blank – no message, no address. Happiness touches me. Somehow I know that the empty white space is a very good thing.

'Nate and I adopted Helen,' I think. 'And then decades later, Gran adopted me.' I smile. It feels like everything is exactly as it should be.

Nate watches me. He puts his hands in his back pockets. "I've, um … always liked the name Helen," he says as I put the postcard away.

"Me too," I say. Then I remember something else I found out from the old newspapers, and I clear my throat. "And … after we adopt her, we'll go on to have two sons of our own."

I feel a little shy. I'm not sure why – this boy and I have been almost as intimate as it's possible for two people to be. But still, talking about our future children makes my cheeks go warm.

Nate looks embarrassed too, but he smiles. "Three children sounds perfect," he says.

I grin. "I'm glad you think so. It's kind of already been decided."

We hold hands and start walking again. When we come to the old house where we met, we glance at each other – and then climb over the fence and drop to the ground.

Inside the house it's dark and shadowy, but it feels friendly. So much has happened here.

Nate stands looking at me. "I was wrong," he says. "I can't tell you how glad I am that I came here that day, Iris. It's when I really started to live."

"Me too," I whisper.

I put my arms around his neck. Though the kiss stays gentle, it reminds me of a hundred others – of the warm weight of his body on mine in bed – the way his hands and mouth make me shiver with desire.

When the kiss ends I smile. "I wonder what it will be like to live with your parents," I say. I know, of course, that we'll be in separate bedrooms there.

Nate winces. "Frustrating," he says.

I trace my finger along his chest. "Oh, like sleeping in the same bed wasn't frustrating?"

"I know." Nate hesitates. "Iris, listen – I've been thinking about that. I brought something from your time ..." He puts his hand in his jeans pocket. Then he frowns and searches his other pocket. He stares at me.

"They're gone," he says.

"What are?"

His cheeks redden. "The box of condoms," he says.

I bought the condoms when Nate and I first got the apartment – before I knew how he felt about waiting until we're married. I go very still. "Oh," I say at last. Then I clear my throat. "Don't you have them in 1922?"

Nate strokes my arms. "Yeah," he says softly. "We do."

I want to make love with him so much that I feel dizzy. Even so, I pause before I reply. When

I do, I hear myself say, "But … I think we should wait."

Nate blinks. "You do?"

I nod and take his hands. I know this is right.

"We're in your time, now," I tell him. "Our time, I mean. Let's do things the way we're supposed to."

Nate gazes down at me. Finally he smiles. "You're right," he says. "But that's not going to make it any easier." Then he grins. "What are your thoughts on getting married young?"

I grin, too. "I'm in favour of it," I say.

"I'm very glad to hear it."

Nate puts his arm around me and we leave the house. It's sunset, and the scent of orange blossoms is heavy in the air.

Somehow I know that we won't be coming back.

When we reach Nate's house, it looks just as I remember – a ranch house with daffodils in the front yard and a mailbox that says 'Baxter'. Nate lets out a breath. I can see his relief at being back here.

I start to ask him what he thinks it will be like, being in this time when we know so much about the future ... and then I frown. *Do* we know about the future? I have a vague idea that there are wars – that bad things happen – but it's all starting to feel like a dream. It's as if this time really *is* where I belong.

It always was.

'Mel knew,' I think in wonder. Who was she, anyway? She acted crazy, but maybe her gift was being able to tune into truths that others couldn't. Or maybe, just maybe, we had a *good* spirit on our side for a change.

The idea makes me smile. 'Thanks, Mel,' I think. And even though she hasn't been born yet, I have the strange sense that she's happy for us.

Nate kisses the side of my head. "Are you ready?" he says.

I lift my chin. "Ready."

We go to the front door. Nate opens it and we step inside. He still has his arm around me. "Mom? Dad?" he calls.

Ruth appears. Her long blond hair is loose and she has on a blue dress. "Boy, are you in trouble," she tells Nate cheerfully. "You're an hour late for dinner!" Then she stares at him. "Why are you dressed like that?"

I can't believe it. An hour late for dinner? So much has happened, but Nate hasn't been gone any time at all.

Nate looks dazed too. "Uh ... it was just for a joke," he tells his sister.

Ruth studies me. "Who's this?" she asks Nate. "Your *girlfriend?*" Her smile is impish.

"Hi, Ruth," I say. "I like your hair that way, instead of in plaits."

Her eyebrows fly up. "How do you know I usually wear plaits?" she demands.

Nate grins and squeezes his sister's shoulders. "Wouldn't you like to know," he teases. I can tell how happy he is. I am, too. As his dark eyes meet mine, it feels like a caress.

Maybe we can't stop his family from being sad. Maybe those things will still happen anyway. But at least now we can love each other without guilt.

Mrs Baxter comes into the front hallway then. She's followed by a tall man who looks a little like Nate. Mrs Baxter gives me a curious look, as if she thinks she remembers me but isn't sure.

This is home now. I know it as well as I know what Nate is going to say next.

He stands up straight, and his arm around me tightens. "Mom ... Dad," he says. "I'd like you to meet Iris – the girl of my dreams."

Our books are tested
for children and young people by
children and young people.

Thanks to everyone who consulted on
a manuscript for their time and effort in
helping us to make our books better
for our readers.

❧About the Author❧

Lee Weatherly was born in the USA in Little Rock, Arkansas. She was the youngest of three children and grew up in a house full of books. She always wanted to be a writer but had lots of other jobs first. Her favourite job was as a hostess at a ski resort – despite the fact she didn't know how to ski. She is very happy to be a writer now so she can work from home in her pyjamas if she wants to!

Lee has lived in the UK for almost 20 years. She lives in Hampshire with her husband and cat and goes for long walks and reads a lot. She's always been interested in Los Angeles and the idea of time travel ... so she couldn't resist writing about Iris and Nate, and thanks Barrington Stoke for making it happen.